Micha Archer

Yanitzia Canetti

# Wonder
# Walkers
# Caminantes
# curiosos

# Dedicated to Leyla, mi amiga buena
## Dedicado a Leyla, mi amiga buena

Nancy Paulsen Books
An imprint of Penguin Random House LLC, New York

Visit us online at penguinrandomhouse.com • Library of Congress Cataloging-in-Publication Data
Names: Archer, Micha, author, illustrator. | Title: Wonder walkers / Micha Archer. | Description: New York: Nancy Paulsen
Books, [2021] | Summary: "Two curious children go for a walk, asking imaginative questions about the natural beauty
that surrounds them"–Provided by publisher. | Identifiers: LCCN 2020019300 | ISBN 9780593109649 (hardcover)
ISBN 9780593109663 (ebook) | ISBN 9780593109656 (ebook) | Subjects: CYAC: Nature–Fiction.
Classification: LCC PZ7.1.A728 Wo 2021 | DDC [E]–dc23 | LC record available at https://lccn.loc.gov/2020019300
Manufactured in China • Special Markets ISBN 9780593531150 • Not for resale • 10 9 8 7 6 5 4 3
Design by Eileen Savage. Text set in a song for jennifer. • The illustrations were done in inks and collage, using tissue
paper and patterned papers created with homemade stamps.

Micha Archer

Traducción de Yanitzia Canetti

# Wonder
# Walkers
# Caminantes
# *curiosos*

Nancy Paulsen Books

Wonder walk?
¿Un paseo curioso?

Sure.

Claro que sí.

Is the sun the
world's light bulb?

¿Es el sol la
bombilla del mundo?

Is fog the river's blanket?

¿Es la niebla el manto del río?

Do mountains have bones?
Are forests the mountain's fur?

¿Tienen huesos las montañas?
¿Son los bosques su pelaje?

I wonder.

Me pregunto.

Me too.

También yo.

Are trees
the sky's legs?

¿Son los árboles
las piernas
del cielo?

Are branches
trees' arms?

¿Son las ramas
los brazos de
los árboles?

Is dirt the world's skin?
¿Es la tierra la piel del mundo?

Are roots the plant's toes?
¿Son las raíces los pies de la planta?

Do caves have mouths?

¿Tienen bocas las cavernas?

Are shells the shore's necklace?
Is the ocean the world's bath?

¿Son las conchas marinas
el collar de las costas?
¿Es el océano la bañera
del mundo?

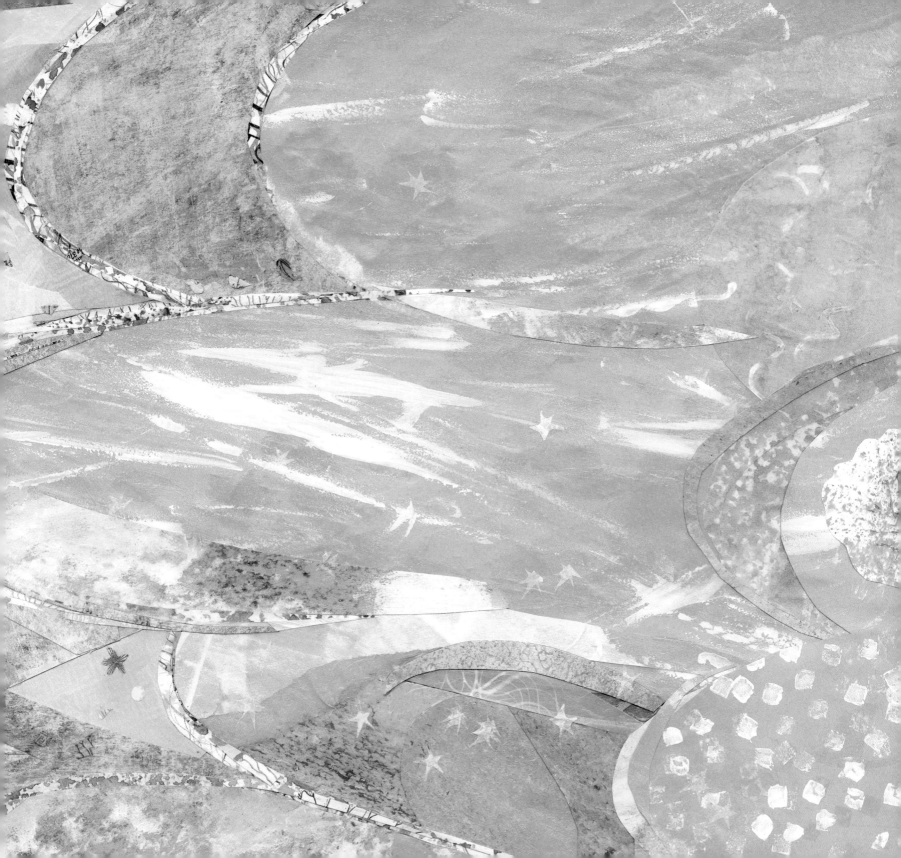

Are rivers the earth's veins?
¿Son los ríos las venas de la tierra?

Is the wind the
world breathing?

¿Es el viento el
mundo respirando?

Is rain the day's tears?

¿Es la lluvia las
lágrimas del día?

Is the moon the world's night-light?

¿Es la luna la luz nocturna del mundo?

I wonder.

Me pregunto.

Me too.

También yo.